# Yum!Yum!!

## Delicious Nursery Rhymes

# Joanne Fitzgerald

# Yum!Yum!!

## Delicious Nursery Rhymes

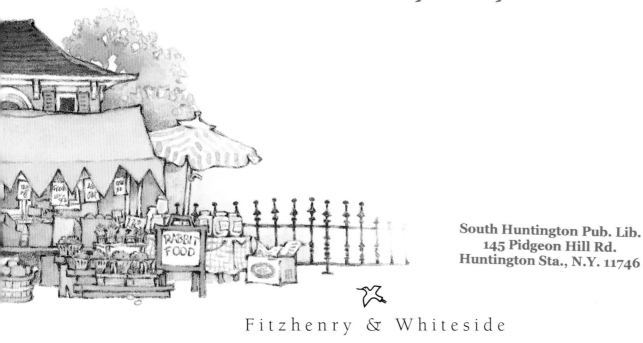

Fitzhenry & Whiteside

Published in Canada by Fitzhenry & Whiteside, 195 Allstate Parkway, Markham, Ontario L3R 4T8
Published in the United States by Fitzhenry & Whiteside, 311 Washington Street, Brighton, Massachusetts 02135

10 9 8 7 6 5 4 3 2 1

**Library and Archives Canada Cataloguing in Publication**
Fitzgerald, Joanne, 1956-
Yum! Yum!! / Joanne Fitzgerald ; illustrated by Joanne Fitzgerald.
ISBN-13: 978-1-55041-888-0     ISBN-10: 1-55041-888-2
1. Food—Juvenile poetry.  I. Title.
PS8611.I89Y84 2008          jC811'.54          C2006-906866-6

Fitzhenry & Whiteside acknowledges with thanks the Canada Council for the Arts, and the Ontario Arts Council
for their support of our publishing program. We acknowledge the financial support of the Government of Canada
through the Book Publishing Industry Development Program (BPIDP) for our publishing activities.

**U.S. Publisher Cataloging-in-Publication Data**
**(Library of Congress Standards)**
Fitzgerald, Joanne.
Yum! Yum!! : Delicious Nursery Rhymes / Joanne Fitzgerald.
[32] p. : col. ill. ;  cm.
Summary: A collection of traditional nursery rhymes about food, set in a farmer's market.
ISBN-10: 1-55041-888-2    ISBN-13: 978-1-55041-888-0
1. Nursery rhymes.  I. Title.
398.8  dc22  PZ8.3.F589 2008

Design by Wycliffe Smith
Printed in Hong Kong

*For farmers everywhere, with many, many thanks for all the wonderful things you grow.*
—J.F.

This little piggy went to market.
This little piggy stayed home.
This little piggy had roast beef.
This little piggy had none.
And this little piggy
Cried *wee-wee-wee*
All the way home.

# Little Tommy Tucker

Sings for his supper.

What shall he eat?

White bread and butter.

How will he cut it

Without a knife?

How will he be married

Without a wife?

# Higgledy, piggledy, my black hen,

She lays eggs for gentlemen.
Gentlemen come every day
To see what my black hen doth lay.
Sometimes nine and sometimes ten,
Higgledy, piggledy, my black hen.

# Little Jack Horner

Sat in a corner

Eating a fresh-baked pie.

He put in his thumb

And pulled out a plum,

And said, "What a good boy am I!"

P olly, put the kettle on,
Polly, put the kettle on,
Polly, put the kettle on;
And we'll all have tea.
Sukey, take it off again,
Sukey, take it off again,
Sukey, take it off again;
They're all gone away.

SNACKS

HOT CHOCOLATE
CANDY
APPLES
·CUPCAKES
·TARTLETS
·COOKIES

# Little Miss Muffet

Sat on a tuffet,

Eating her curds and whey.

Along came a spider,

Who sat down beside her,

And frightened Miss Muffet away.

**P**eter Piper picked a peck of pickled peppers.
A peck of pickled peppers Peter Piper picked.
If Peter Piper picked a peck of pickled peppers,
Where's the peck of pickled peppers Peter Piper
picked?

**P**ease porridge hot,
Pease porridge cold,
Pease porridge in the pot
Nine days old.
Some like it hot,
Some like it cold,
Some like it in the pot
Nine days old.

9
DAYS
OLD

PEASE
PORRIDGE

SM LG

HOT .50 .75

COLD .35 .50

OLD 75 .95

Really Old .05

Jack Sprat could eat no fat.
His wife could eat no lean.
And so, between them both, you see,
They licked the platter clean.

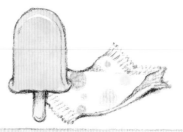

I eat my peas with honey.
I've done it all my life.
It makes the peas taste funny,
But it keeps them on the knife.

If all the world were apple pie,
And all the sea were ink,
And all the trees were bread and cheese,
What should we have to drink?

I had a little nut tree.
Nothing would it bear
But a silver nutmeg
And a golden pear.
The king of Spain's daughter
Came to visit me,
All for the sake
Of my little nut tree.

Sunflowers
$3.99
Mixed Bouquets
$2.99

leafy
vetch

night night